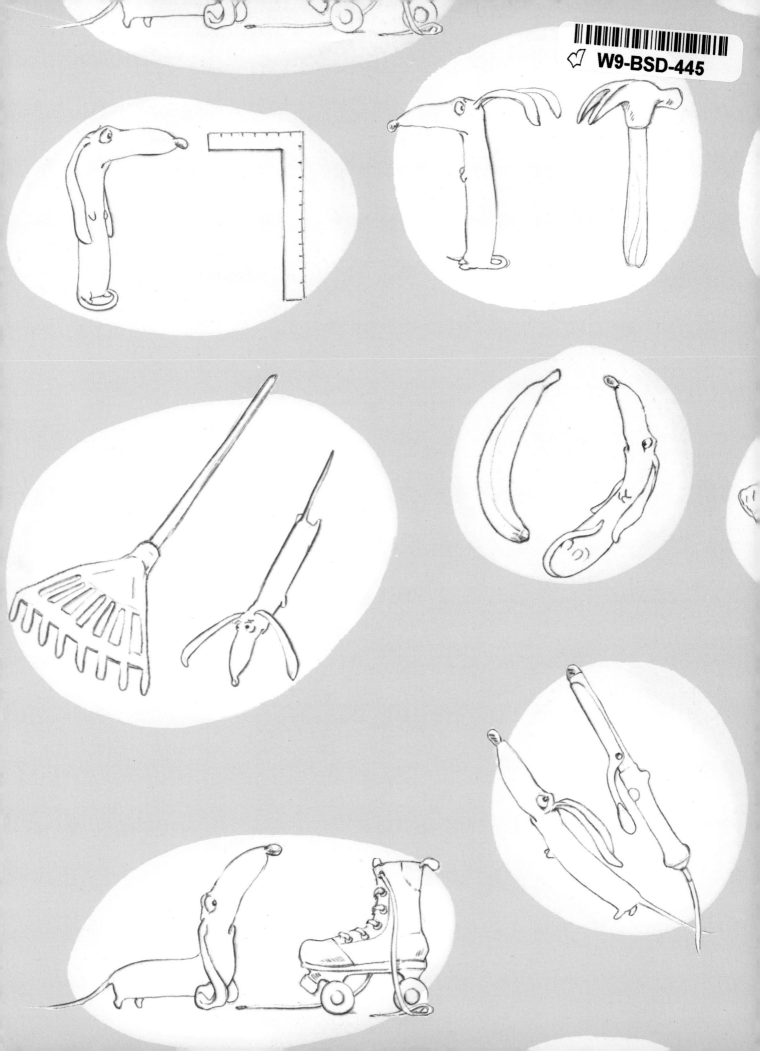

Sterling, ~~Best Fork~~ Dog Ever

Aidan Cassie

FARRAR STRAUS GIROUX / New York

BUTLERY CUTLERY CO.

For Maia—
Often unusual, always herself

Farrar Straus Giroux Books for Young Readers
An imprint of Macmillan Publishing Group, LLC
175 Fifth Avenue, New York, NY 10010

Copyright © 2018 by Aidan Cassie
Color separations by Embassy Graphics
Printed in China by Toppan Leefung Printing Ltd.,
Dongguan City, Guangdong Province
First edition, 2018
10 9 8 7 6 5 4 3 2 1
mackids.com

Library of Congress Control Number: 2017956978
ISBN: 978-0-374-30614-4

Our books may be purchased in bulk for promotional, educational, or business use. Please
contact your local bookseller or the Macmillan Corporate and Premium Sales Department at
(800) 221-7945 ext. 5442 or by e-mail at MacmillanSpecialMarkets@macmillan.com.

Sterling slept in a mostly waterproof box on a slightly damp pillow. It was like a house. But not much like a home. No home had wanted to keep Sterling, not for long.

This time will be different, he thought.
I'll *be different*.

The next day, the Butlery Cutlery Company
delivered Sterling, on time and undamaged,
to the Gilberts' front door.

Inside his box, Sterling tried to be as silver and straight as he could (though parts of him wriggled quite uncontrollably).

Clearly, he was a fork.

He was not, however, what the Gilberts had ordered.

"I suppose we could keep him," said the father. "He *is* very small."

"And very quiet," noted the mother.

"And the very most adorable thing ever!"
said the girl.

It seemed that Sterling could stay.

And this time he would make sure he stayed for good. He would be handy. And useful. He would be everything the Gilberts wanted in a fork.
He'd be the best fork ever!

Only, forks do not walk on leashes.

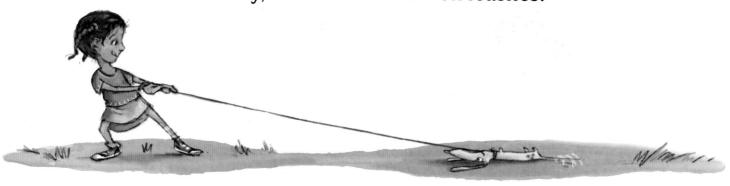

They do not sit.

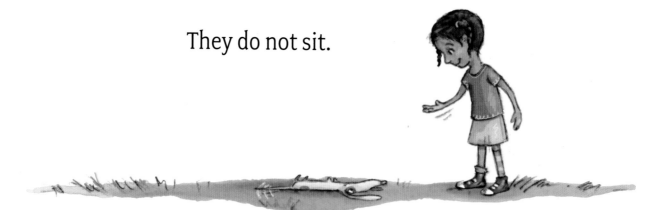

They do not fetch.

And forks never sleep on beds. Sterling was sure of it.

One evening, when he saw the family eat an entire meal with just their fingers, he began to wonder . . .

What if they don't even need a fork?

Maybe they needed a better whisk.

He'd be perfect for pastry.

Sterling was adaptable.

However, Mr. and Mrs. Gilbert
were not impressed. Not at all.

The next morning, the girl took Sterling out,
though he couldn't imagine why. He would be the best
whatever-she-needed, if she'd just take him back home.

Instead, they stopped beside a meadow filled with creatures wiggling and waggling, fetching and frolicking.

"Go on," said the girl. "Go play."
It did look like fun. Maybe the girl wanted
him to be . . .

A STICK!

That night, as everyone
got ready for bed,

Sterling didn't know
where he belonged.

Not at all.

He wanted to make the girl
happy, but he didn't know how.
Then, he saw it. It had been in
front of him the whole time.

Sterling leaped onto the girl's bed and into her arms. He could see it in her eyes; she just wanted him to be *himself*.

She didn't need him to be a fork or a whisk, a stick or a log. Clearly, he was just Sterling: the huggable, snuggable, perfectly lovable dog.

And sometimes pillow.

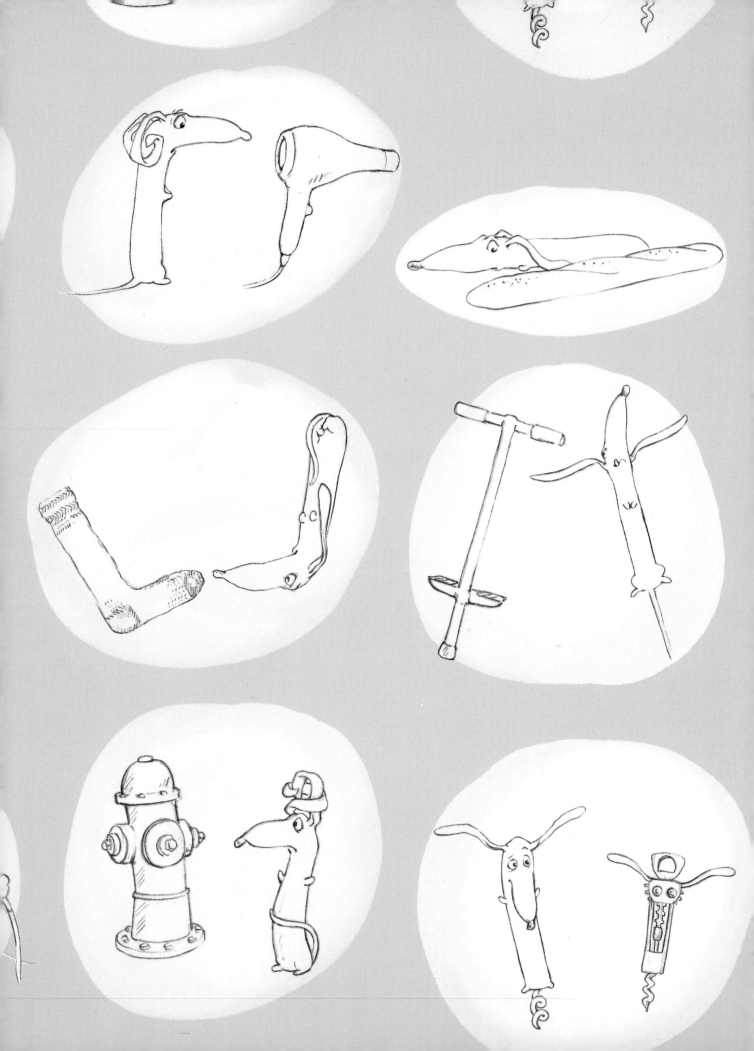